Max, the Music-Maker

by MIRIAM B. STECHER
and ALICE S. KANDELL

Lothrop, Lee & Shepard Books   New York

For Andrew Joseph

Library of Congress Cataloging in Publication Data
Stecher, Miriam B
Max, the music-maker.
SUMMARY: Max find music everywhere—in the roar
of a train, in the purr of a pussycat, and in the
instruments he makes himself.
[1. Music—Fiction] I. Kandell, Alice S.,
joint author. I. Title.
PZ7.S8135Max [E] 80-10692
ISBN 0-688-41958-5
ISBN 0-688-51958-X lib. bdg.

Max finds music
sounds all about,
indoors or out.
He clicks a stick
against a fence,
making music for
a walk.

The subway grate
sings bimble-dee-bim,
and Max sings it too.
When he hears a train
roar in, Max roars
right back.

His ears can hear
the softest of sounds,
like the pur-r-ing
pussycat…

...or insects in the grass.

Max plays music sounds on things he finds
or makes. Some of them he taps…

...and some
of them he
shakes.

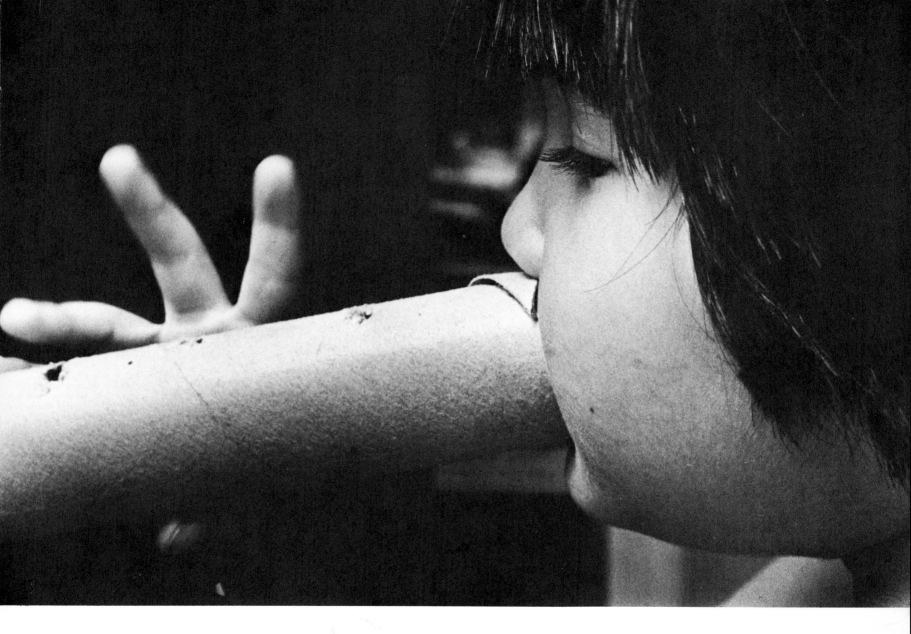

Once he made some tooters out of cardboard tubes.

When friends came by to visit,
they took turns being the leader of the band.

Sometimes Max likes loud sounds,
but other people don't.

"Ouch," they say. "Please don't play that way!"

Once he tried out pot lids, crashing them together many times.

"That makes my ears hurt too," sighed Max.
"I'll have to look for other ways to play."

Soon he discovered that pot lids make
a ringing, singing sound when
tapped together very lightly.

One day Dad took Max to a music show to hear a grownup musician play.

Their seats were so far back they could hardly see the stage, but the music sounded fine.

During intermission he got a closer look
and a chance to try the strings of a komungo.

When Max came home, he made a rubberbandjo.

Then he found a board and pretended
to make music on it.

Dad helped him cut some fishing line for strings.
A small piece of wood made a "bridge."
Now Max can put on his own music show.

Max sings songs too. Sometimes he sings while pretending he can fly, or...

that he's a singer on TV. Some of the
songs he sings are glad and some are sad.

Sleepy songs for Snoopy don't
need any words. Just hums
and secret whisperings till no
more sounds are heard, except…

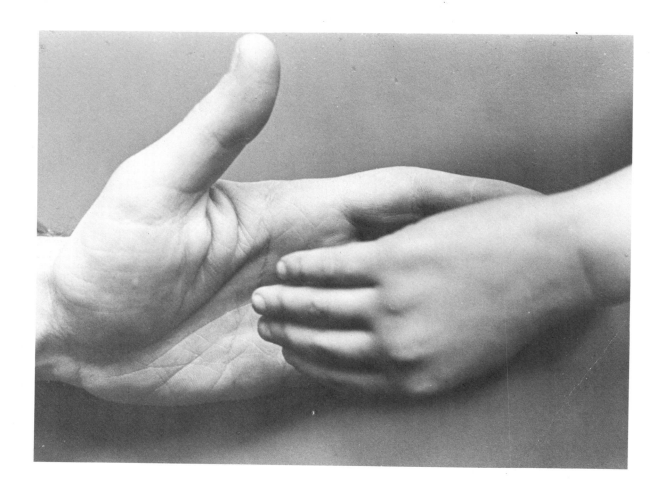

Good night, Dad.
Good night, Max.

MIRIAM B. STECHER is music/dance/dramatics specialist at the Horace Mann School for the Nursery Years in New York City. The idea for *Max, the Music-Maker* is the result of her many years of work with young children.

DR. ALICE S. KANDELL, psychologist, photographer, and a parent at the Horace Mann School, at Miriam Stecher's suggestion photographed her son while he was absorbed in creative work/play and unaware of her special purposes.

Together, Mrs. Stecher and Dr. Kandell have created a book that shows a child busy at creative music-making—before taking lessons. Mrs. Stecher believes it is important for adults to encourage young children to satisfy their natural curiosity about interesting sounds in playful, nondirected ways. This will "open" their ears, sharpening listening skills and developing important music and science concepts, and is the best possible preparation for formal education when the child is older.